HUMAN UNFORGIVEN

HUMAN UNFORGIVEN

K. R. WATTS

STUART TARTLY PRESS

Stuart Tartly Press
17216 Saticoy Street, #226
Lake Balboa, CA 91406-2103

ISBN: 978-1-953595-05-8

CONTENTS

For all those who have believed themselves doomed.

Religion is regarded by the common people as true, by
the wise as false, and by the rulers as useful.

— Seneca 4 BC -AD 65

LOVE, DEATH, AND SIN

Chapter 1

"We have few records of Adam Kinde's years in seminary. At seventeen he was a witness in an inquiry into the moral character of the seminary chaplain. At nineteen he was returned to the seminary one night in an inebriated state by the local police. Beyond that, we must deduce what we can from other sources."

Silas Redford,
The Real Adam Kinde: An Experiment in Biography

IT WAS the week after I committed the unforgivable sin—and the week before the body was found.

Dolores Thomas tugged at my sleeve on the way to student chapel. I caught a whiff of her perfume, so I knew it was her before I turned.

"Would you do something for me, Adam?"

We both knew the answer to that.

Mr. Matthews, my history teacher, told us about a kind of morality tale that was prevalent toward the end of the Dark Age—in the dispensation just prior to the second coming of Joshua and his thousand-year reign. It was called "film noir" and was based on the story of Adam and Eve in the Bible.

The stories were all different, but basically they were tragedies, each tracing the fall and destruction of a man because he was seduced by the charms of a woman.

I'm not saying that Dolores is a "femme fatale" (that's what the women in those stories were called), but there was something about her that reminds me of those morality tales.

I was seventeen at the time, and Dolores was sixteen, going on twenty-five.

She *was* my Eve in one way—the same way she was for every boy in the seminary.

She was the only girl in our world.

Her father, Dr. Thomas, was the head of the lower school, and Dolores had had the run of the place since she was old enough to run.

But she had just recently become conscious of her effect on the young men who filled its halls, and she couldn't resist experimenting. She had a way of looking you in the eyes that was very unnerving, and she enjoyed using it.

It worked, even on me—even though I had no interest in her romantically. She could still make me blush at twenty paces with a single inappropriately intimate glance. It had an even stronger effect on the half of the student body who were secretly in love with her.

But she wasn't playing that game just then. I could tell by her tone that she was in her other role, the one I was more familiar with—and much more comfortable with as well.

She was in "little sister" mode, wanting to cry on my shoulder, or confide in me, or ask for my help.

I stepped out of the herd of students moving toward chapel

and led her through a stone archway into the cooler air of an alcove, ignoring the jealous glances I received.

"What's the matter?" I asked.

She wrinkled her nose at me.

"You're friends with Flash, right?"

Flash Andrews was a year older than me, quarterback on our football team, one of the stars in the school constellation. He was arrogant, and a bit of a bully. My connection with him was complicated.

"We're friendly enough."

"Oh. Well, I mean… Would he *talk* to you? About personal stuff?"

I didn't like where this was going.

"I don't know," I said. "Why?"

"I was, just—just hoping you could find something out for me."

"Like what?"

I'd guessed already, but I wanted to be wrong.

"I was wondering if you could find out if he—if he has… if he's *noticed* me."

"You're the only girl on campus. Everybody's noticed you."

"Yeah, but I mean…"

I frowned.

"You mean is he interested in you. Romantically."

She blushed and nodded.

THE FIRST TIME I saw Flash Andrews he was torturing an angel.

Back home, on the Franklyn estate where my father worked and my family lived, the very idea of an angel had been a source of awe to me.

I had only seen one ever, and then only caught a glimpse of it through the branches of a tree, but it had been a critical moment. It was the reason I chose to go to seminary when I was offered the chance. I wanted desperately to learn as much as I could about the part of creation that held such wonders.

But I was soon to learn, once I arrived at the seminary, that angels could be mundane to the point of boredom. Or at least Dr. Thomas' guardian angel was. Dr. Thomas mostly used it to summon students to his office, so we saw a lot of it, which was one reason it quickly lost its magic for us.

Supernatural being or not, you can't appear day after day to a group of young boys with the same deep intonation of "FEAR NOT!" on your tongue without becoming a target of humor.

By the second week we had lost all sense of awe. By the third week, the idea that there was anything to fear about the creature was ludicrous. By the fourth week the humorists among us were getting predictable laughs by intoning "Fear Not!" from the back of the classroom.

And, of course, angels are the most humorless and the most literal of all of God's creations. That, in itself, was enough to make this one an object of fun.

But while we might have stifled a giggle or two in the angel's presence, none of us were likely to actually be cruel to the poor thing.

Except Flash.

I was on my way to class one morning and rounded a corner just in time to see the angel shimmer into existence in front of Flash and a couple of his friends. They were older students, so I backed off and watched from a distance—not wanting to call attention to myself.

"FEAR NOT! Flash Andrews, your presence is required at—"

"Oooowahhhhh!"

Something halfway between a deep moan and a terrified scream emerged from Flash's mouth, and he staggered backwards, his arm covering his face.

His friends exchanged amused glances.

The angel stopped mid-sentence, assessed the situation, and changed tactics.

"There is no need to fear, Flash Andrews. I will not harm—"

Flash screamed again, then cowered.

"Don't kill me! Please! Let me live!"

The angel was silent for a moment, then tried again, in a quieter voice.

"You are safe in my presence, Flash Andrews. You need not—"

Flash pushed one of his friends toward the angel.

"Here. You can kill *him*. Just please leave me alone!"

The angel was silent again for a time, then apparently decided to cut to the chase.

"Please report to the head of school."

Flash lowered his arm, feigning amazement.

"That's all?"

"That is all," the angel said. "There was no need to fear—"

Flash interrupted.

"Why did you have to *threaten* me like that?" he demanded.

His friends were in hysterics.

The angel was clearly confused.

"I did not threaten—"

"You should be ashamed of yourself, terrorizing a mere mortal."

"I did not intend—"

But Flash cut him off.

"Tell the head I'll be right there."

The angel stared at him for a moment in confusion, then simply vanished.

Flash and his friends fell over each other laughing.

I felt sorry for the angel.

As I followed the crowd into chapel I spotted a couple of the youngest students at the windows near the balcony entrance above me, watching Dr. Thomas crossing the pond from his residence.

I remembered doing the same thing my first year.

Like angels, walking on water loses its magic after you've seen it enough. But it never became an object of fun. Dr. Thomas was not the sort of person you make fun of.

He was kind and fair, but also clearly in charge. We respected him.

I'd often wondered why he chose to cross that pond on foot on his way to chapel. There were much easier ways, especially if the weather was cold or windy or raining. He could easily have walked the sheltered path around the pond, or even used his chariot.

I suspected it was for the benefit of those younger students who pass that window on their way to chapel. But I wasn't sure why he thought that was a good idea. And I wasn't convinced that the idea was just his alone, either. It could hardly have been a coincidence that that particular window, right by the entrance to the balcony and with a view of the pond, was the only one that wasn't made of stained glass on that whole side of the building.

Another time I might have puzzled over that straight through the chapel service. But my promise to Dolores was weighing heavily on me.

The truth was, I didn't want to get involved.

I steered clear of Flash and his gang for the most part until I was fifteen. My friends got dumped head-first into trash cans, crammed forcibly into their own cubbies, and tortured generally, but I managed to keep a low profile and a safe distance.

Then one day I made the mistake of being the last of my class to leave the changing room after physical education class.

My cubby was toward the end of one of the changing aisles, against a wall, and Flash appeared with Eddie White—one of his more violent friends—at the other end.

I was trapped.

Flash and Eddie and a couple of others called themselves "The Order of the Sword." I don't think it was actually anything as organized as a club. But they all hung around together, and did things like terrorizing the younger boys or taunting the head's angel.

I thought there was just a chance that they might let me past them if I did nothing to call attention to myself. So I finished dressing without looking up, stowed my workout clothes in my cubby, stood, and walked toward them.

They were both looking right at me, which was not a good sign. My heart was pumping wildly, but I struggled to appear nonchalant, and didn't slow my pace.

As I got close I returned their gaze, forced myself to smile, and nodded.

Eddie stepped in front of me.

I stopped. And even though I knew it was futile I managed to look puzzled.

Eddie just grinned.

"Where do you think you're going?"

"I'm late for Greek class."

I made a half-hearted attempt to move past him.

He shoved me backward with an open hand.

I stepped over the bench that divided the center of the aisle and tried to pass Flash.

He didn't move.

At first.

Then he stepped forward, forcing me to back up.

I tried to keep the puzzled look on my face.

"I'm Adam. Adam Kinde. Can I do something for you guys?"

Eddie just grinned wider.

"We know who you are."

"Look guys, I really need to get to class. So if you could just let me past you..."

Flash looked at Eddie.

"He thinks *he* should be telling *us* what to do."

"No," I said. "I'm just asking."

Eddie frowned.

"So you're calling Flash a liar?"

Flash had a pained expression.

"The kid needs to learn a lesson."

And that was when Eddie drove his fist into my gut.

My legs went out from under me, and I crumpled toward the ground. An arm caught me, and kept me from falling. I couldn't breathe, and everything went dark. I made a kind of gasping whine, but no air got into my lungs.

The arm lowered me to the bench and Flash said, "You're all right. Stay calm. Give it a minute."

After a little while I could get some air into my lungs, and my vision slowly returned. Flash still had an arm around my shoulder.

"Better?"

Eddie was gone.

"Yeah," I said. "I guess."

"You need to see the healer?"

"I'm okay."

"You sure? You want me to walk to class with you?"

"I'm fine."

"Well, listen. Take it slow."

He never asked me not to report him, but I never did. I don't quite know why. But from that day forward I was immune to bullying.

Flash never bullied me again. But neither did his pals, or any of the other students. I think I was under his protection.

Later, he even seemed to think of me as a friend. At first he would brag to me about stuff I didn't approve of—fights he'd been in, trouble he got into, that sort of thing. But as time went by he began including more personal stuff. He even used me as a sounding board, or adviser.

I was used to that role, of course. I don't know how or why, but it seemed like half the students confided their problems to me or asked for my advice. I never encouraged it, but they did.

So I knew two things. The first was that I could find out practically anything Dolores wanted to know about Flash. The second was that I already knew too much about him to think it was a good idea to help her.

Chapter 2

"The primary task of any state religion is to control the worldview of the populace—a task that was greatly simplified because all media during that period were owned and operated by the clergy. And tremendous care was taken in the training of those clergy to cement the desired worldview in their minds."

Lillian Trublood,
The Dynamics of Deception: Indoctrination Method and Practice During the Short Domination

THERE'S something about ritual that puts you in a different place. For just a moment, as I entered the chapel, I forgot about Dolores and Flash and my unforgivable sin.

I had entered that space hundreds of times since I first came to seminary, and just walking in the door awakened a kind of composite memory in me of all those experiences.

It may have been the scent of old wood and candle smoke, or the cool, quiet air, or the music. Tom Brown, an older student and an accomplished musician, was playing the hymn for entering on his harmonica up front, and the high, sweet notes echoed in the vast space above us.

But I think it was also some homier and plainer things: the threadbare rug on the floor just inside the entrance, the subdued voices of the students in the pews, the watchful eyes of the teachers monitoring our entrance.

I made my way to my seat, traced a circle on the front of my Bible, and the first hymn appeared on its surface, matching the number on the hymn board that hung to the right of the pulpit.

That was another of the mysteries of the seminary—like Dr. Thomas' walk across the lake. The hymn board was a throwback to the Dark Age, a sort of frame with grooved spaces to hold wooden cards with numbers on them. Each time we had chapel, someone (I suppose it was Pastor Dean) manually changed the cards so that the board displayed a list of the hymns we'd be singing. He did the same for the scripture board on the other side, which displayed the verse references for the sermon.

Like Dr. Thomas' walk across the lake, there was no practical reason for him to go to all that trouble. Every student had a Bible which displayed the correct hymns and scripture, so the point of those boards escaped me.

Like I said: a mystery.

We stood to sing the first hymn, and Pastor Dean opened with prayer. It was a Thursday, so the youngest class filed forward then, for the blessing of their Bibles. After the second hymn he called three of the oldest boys forward for a culmination ceremony.

They were being ordained to the seminary proper, to their final studies toward ministry.

The three came and knelt on the step to the platform, and

Pastor Dean turned his back to us and faced the cabinet which hangs on the wall behind the pulpit. It contains the lamp and the sword—the two symbols of the seminary.

He made the same sign of the stone you use on your Bible, and the cabinet door swung open. He took the oil lamp in one hand and the sword in the other and carried them to the communion table in front of the pulpit, where he laid the sword.

He then lit the lamp, stepped forward, dipped a finger in the oil, and touched it to the first boy's forehead, anointing him with the oil of the spirit.

He did this to each of them, then put the lamp on the table. Then, lifting the two-edged sword of the word, he tapped each of them on each shoulder.

This was done in complete silence, and we all hardly breathed while it was happening. One day we would be kneeling where those boys were now, and the solemnity of the moment was not lost on any of us.

We sang the third hymn, and it was time for the sermon.

Dr. Thadeus Miller was preaching on Thursdays that month.

I'VE HAD MIXED feelings about Dr. Miller since I first met him.

He has a reputation as an excellent teacher, but I've never had a class with him, so I couldn't say about that. Flash, who had him for prolegomena to deep theology, practically worshiped him.

But that was Flash.

As a preacher, he was impressive. His sermons started out quiet, almost conversational. He would even get a few laughs at the start, and generally relaxed the congregation. Then, when he had you hooked, he would slowly build the pressure to a grand crescendo of guilt and fear that made Jonathan Edwards' *Sinners in the Hands of an Angry God* read like a lullaby by comparison.

Not my favorite style of sermon, but he certainly had some skill.

As a person—well, that was where I formed my first impression of him.

I had to get clearance on my school schedule when I was fourteen, and my academic advisor was out with the flu, so I was sent across campus to Dr. Miller's office. Except for the occasional course in deep theology, he taught in the seminary proper, so I had only seen him when he preached in chapel. He opened the door when I knocked and waved me to a seat while talking to someone on his Bible. I couldn't hear the other half of the conversation, but it was apparently another faculty member. They were discussing a recent meeting with Dr. Thomas.

I don't know if it's common for faculty members to ridicule each other in private or not. Maybe it is. But I had great respect for Dr. Thomas, and was thoroughly embarrassed by the way they were talking about him.

I felt like I was the adult and Thadeus Miller was a first-year student making fun of a teacher.

He eventually realized that I couldn't help hearing what he was saying, and what he did then colored the way I've thought of him ever since. He got this smarmy little smirk on his face, looked directly at me, and winked.

I felt dirty, as though I'd been made complicit in something I didn't understand and wanted no part of.

⸻

DR. MILLER'S sermon that Thursday was on the death of Judas.

It was like all of his sermons in that the theme was strict obedience, and his method was to inspire fear and guilt.

I found my mind flitting from the sermon topic to my promise to Dolores, to my great sin, to Flash, and back again.

One way or another, they were all connected.

One reason that I didn't want to help Dolores connect with Flash—the strongest reason if not the most rational one—was that he had committed the same sin I had, but in a way that had to do with her.

FLASH HAD APPROACHED me in the refectory during lunch several days before. He put his tray next to mine, sat down, leaned close, and spoke so low that I could hardly hear him above the lunchtime chatter and clatter of dishes that filled the room.

"I need to ask you something."

I swallowed a mouthful of mashed potatoes and put my fork down.

"Sure. What?"

He glanced around the table at our fellow diners and lowered his voice even more.

"Not here. Later."

We ended up meeting on a bench in the courtyard, the birdsong, greenery, and quiet breezes in sharp contrast to the dark subject we discussed.

He surveyed the garden before beginning.

"Look. This is a really private thing. I can count on you, right?"

"You mean to not go blabbing it all over campus?"

"Yeah. Sorry. I know you wouldn't. It's just…"

A long silence.

"Well?" I asked.

He cleared his throat.

"So you remember Dr. Miller's sermon last week?"

Remember it? I'd been tortured by it. And the last thing I wanted to do was talk about it.

"The one about the unforgivable sin?"

"Right. Well, the thing is, I think I've done it."

I waited.

"So you know Dolores, right? The head's daughter?"

"The only girl on campus?"

"Yeah. Well, I think she's pretty, um... well, attractive. In a kind of very..."

I waited again.

He was actually turning red.

"Well, I... Sometimes, when I'm in bed... and I'm... Well, you know..."

I did know, but I didn't actually want to *hear* about it.

"Sometimes I think about her as I'm... And the thing is, you remember what Dr. Miller said, about *convictions*? Well I think —actually I'm sure—that I had one."

"A conviction?"

"Yeah. Like God... the Holy Spirit, you know... like it was telling me that what I was doing was wrong, and I should stop."

I nodded. He continued.

"So the thing is, I knew it *was* wrong. And I knew I *should* stop. But I kept right on anyway. And I'm pretty sure that's exactly what Dr. Miller was talking about."

"So you think you've committed the unforgivable sin."

He looked absolutely miserable.

"And I don't know what to *do* now. I mean, it's all over, right? I'm going to hell, and I can't even figure out what that means about *now*. Or next week even, you know? I know you think I'm a bit of an asshole, Kinde. But I'm really not that bad. Some people would just figure, well, you know, 'Whoopee! I can sin all I want now, because it doesn't make a difference.' But I don't want to live like that. I'd undo it if I could..."

I didn't know what to tell him, because I was going through the exact same thing.

Chapter 3

"...with the result that some of the more devout adolescents came to believe that they had, in fact, committed this 'unforgivable sin.' For reasons which will be discussed below, this must be considered a side effect of the general indoctrination strategy rather than a conscious goal."

Lillian Trublood,
The Dynamics of Deception: Indoctrination Method and Practice During the Short Domination

WELL, not the *exact* same thing.

I knew well enough what he was talking about, and I have my own sexual fantasies, but it's never occurred to me to include an actual person—one that I *knew*—in them. When he mentioned it to me, it just sounded so disrespectful. So I suppose that's why I never did.

And maybe that's why I never experienced the conviction that he did.

My unforgivable sin had nothing at all to do with sex.

But aside from that, theologically speaking we were definitely in the same boat. The only difference was our point of weakness.

Flash's weakness seemed to be between his legs, while mine was definitely between my ears.

If Flash had been in the garden of Eden, he might have taken a bite of that apple as part of a plan to seduce Eve. I would have bitten it because I absolutely *had* to know what would really happen if I did.

I could never stand a mystery. That clear window by the balcony, the head's habit of walking across the pond, the reason behind the hymn board and the scripture board in the chapel —all of those things bug the heck out of me. I want to understand them, I want to *know*.

Seeing that angel when I was a kid made me so curious I ended up in seminary.

So when I overheard Pastor Dean talking to the head of school one day, in ominous tones, about something called "O.C.S.", I couldn't let it go.

I tried looking it up, but my Bible only has student permissions and I couldn't find anything at all. I asked a couple of older students, and they hadn't heard of it either.

Finally one day I found myself sitting next to Pastor Dean at the table in his office. Dr. Miller was there as well, and another student. We were waiting for the other two student members of the chapel planning committee, so there was nothing going on.

Even so, I probably wouldn't have spoken up, except that Pastor Dean and I have a history. He was the chaplain on the Franklyn estate when I was growing up, he was the only one who ever talked to me about religion as a kid, and it was because of him (and my curiosity) that I came to seminary in the first place.

I was very comfortable talking to him. It was different than talking to any other faculty member.

So we were sitting there, waiting for the rest of the committee, and I decided just to ask him directly.

"What does 'O.C.S.' mean, sir?"

From the shock on his face you would have thought I'd committed heresy.

Dr. Miller's head swiveled in my direction, and he stared first at me and then at Pastor Dean with something between a question and an accusation in his eyes.

Pastor Dean glanced at Dr. Miller sideways, without moving his head, then met my eyes with a seriousness I hadn't witnessed in him before.

"I have no idea," he said. "Ask me later, and we'll look it up together."

His expression left me no doubt that I was to drop the subject immediately.

Luckily, the other two students walked in at that moment, and the meeting started.

After the meeting he asked me if I had heard from my family recently, and listened to my reply while tidying up his office—straightening chairs, sliding his Bible into a desk drawer, rearranging items on a shelf. He kept me talking until Dr. Miller had left. Then he closed the door, and motioned me to a chair. He leaned against the edge of his desk, looking down at me.

"Now, Adam. What was it you tried to ask me just before the meeting?"

He seemed completely relaxed then, all of the shock gone from his face.

I was still nervous.

"I'm sorry sir, if I said something I shouldn't have, but I

overheard you and the head talking the other day—not on purpose, I just happened to—and you were saying something about 'O.C.S.,' and I wondered what that was."

"I see."

He paused for a long moment in thought. After a time, he took a deep breath and spoke.

"I want you to listen to me carefully, Adam. You have, quite inadvertently, trod on some very dangerous ground. There's a good chance it will come to nothing, but I can't be sure. I think you know me well enough to know that I don't countenance lying. But under these very special circumstances that's exactly what I'm going to ask you to do. And I'm going to ask you to do it on my say-so, without any explanation, except that you can trust me that it is the only right and safe course. Can you do that?"

"I think so, sir."

"Not good enough, I'm afraid. I need your absolute promise."

I wasn't at all comfortable with that, but this was Pastor Dean.

I nodded.

"Yes sir. I promise sir."

"Hmm. Alright then. Here's what I want you to do. Forget that you ever heard that conversation between me and the head. Hopefully, that will be the end of the matter. But there is just a chance that Dr. Miller, or someone he tells about your question, will ask you about it. If that happens, you are to say that you heard someone mention it... um, in the refectory, I think, during breakfast. You didn't see who it was, but are pretty sure it was another student. You'd never heard of it before, so you asked me before the meeting. You asked me again, after the meeting, and I tried to look it up for you, but couldn't find anything."

He paused for a moment, replaying what he had just said in his head, then gave a nod, as though it had passed some test.

"Do you think *you* can do that?"

"I think so. I mean, yes sir, I can."

"If you *do* get questioned, don't spill it all out like a memorized speech. Just answer whatever questions they ask you, but stick to that story. And that's *all* you know about it."

"Yes sir."

His manner softened again.

"I'm so sorry you got sucked into this, Adam."

"I shouldn't have been listening, sir."

"Possibly. But I should have been more cautious, as well. Don't be too worried. There's a very good chance that this is the last you'll hear of it."

But of course it wasn't.

I don't mean that Dr. Miller pulled me in for questioning. He didn't. And no one else did either.

But I couldn't leave that apple alone.

Mr. Matthews—the history teacher who told us about film noir—gave us a research assignment about the Dark Age. For purposes of the assignment he relaxed some of the restrictions on our Bibles, allowing us access to some of the Dark Age archives with strict instructions that we were only to investigate our approved research topic and nothing else.

I hadn't been doing the research for more than five minutes when I realized that O.C.S. might have something to do with the Dark Age, and this might be my chance to find out.

I set up a search for O.C.S. and immediately had a deep conviction that I shouldn't go any further.

I wish I had heard Flash's story before this happened, because I might have stopped there if I had. But I hadn't, and I wasn't thinking about the unforgivable sin.

Nevertheless, I *did* have the conviction. I did realize that what

I was about to do was unquestionably wrong in so many ways—not just a breaking of the rules about access, or even the teacher's explicit instructions about the limits of our research, but much more than that. I was breaking my promise to Pastor Dean, letting him down, and quite possibly stirring up more trouble.

But I was curious.

So I did it anyway.

And it was all for nothing, which just made it worse. Oh, I found lots of possibilities. A source from the period called "Wikipedia" had a whole list. "Outer Continental Shelf," "Obsessive Compulsive Syndrome," "Officer Candidate School," and many others. But none of them were the kind of thing that would have created the reaction I got from Pastor Dean and Dr. Miller.

The further down the list I went, the guiltier I felt. But my curiosity wasn't exhausted until I'd eaten the whole apple—stem and seeds included.

And then, of course, remorse.

And after that, the realization that I had just done what Dr. Miller had described in his sermon. I had rejected the conviction of the Holy Spirit.

I had committed the unforgivable sin.

So I knew exactly what Flash was talking about.

One moment your biggest worry is whether you'll be prepared for that test or whether you'll perform well in the next track meet, and the next moment the entire meaning of your life is in question.

You might think I was mostly worried about going to Hell after I died, but oddly that wasn't what bothered me. I hardly thought about that, and I doubt it was the first concern for Flash, either.

Ever since I had made the decision to go to seminary, my connection to God had been a basic part of who I was. All those hours of worship, of prayer, of Bible study, had become such a part of me that I couldn't imagine who I was without that connection. It had become the source of all meaning to me.

And living up to all that—which was, I guess, the same as 'being good'—was the central purpose of life for me.

The idea of having cut myself off from it all, of being cut off from God, was like being cut off from myself. It felt empty, numb, purposeless, and meaningless. Cut off from everything that was good in the world.

There was no longer any point in doing the right thing, or caring for others, or telling the truth, or any of the other virtues. I might still *do* some of those things, out of habit, but it no longer mattered. There was no point in anything.

I was a lost soul. And that seemed much worse than any physical pain I could imagine after death.

I didn't know how to go on.

THOSE OLD HABITS DID PREVAIL, though. I half-promised to help Dolores, though I didn't want to. I listened to Flash's agony even though I didn't know how to make it better. And I tried to help young Arthur.

Arthur was a year younger than me, and far more innocent. In his first two years he had been one of Flash's favorite victims, and he still resented that.

And he was in love—or, at the very least, head-over-heels infatuated.

With Dolores, of course.

He had it bad. And he kept asking me the same sort of questions Dolores asked about Flash. Had she said anything about him? Did I think she knew he existed? Could I, maybe, just put in a word for him?

His latest requests had come shortly after Dolores asked me to help her with Flash, and I had tried to let him down easy.

"There's always a *chance*, Arthur. But I honestly don't think it's a big one. She has her pick of half the boys in the school."

"So what should I do to, you know, improve the odds?"

"You're asking the wrong person. I probably know less about romance than you do."

"But she *talks* to you."

"As a friend. That's all. If I were interested in her the way you are, I wouldn't stand a chance."

He got all thoughtful.

"You're sure you really *aren't* interested, in that way?"

I laughed.

"I'm sure."

"You wouldn't just be trying to discourage me, because I'm competition?"

"No, Arthur. I'm not."

"Then why won't you help me?"

I sighed.

"For lots of reasons."

"Like what?"

"To start with, I don't know how."

"You could think of *something*."

"Even if I did, it might backfire and make things even worse."

"I'd take the chance."

"It's just not how those things work, Arthur."

"Then tell *me* what to do."

I relented, a little.

"I don't know. Find some way to introduce yourself. Figure out something she's interested in, and get to know her."

He brightened.

"Like what?"

"Look, Arthur. I really don't think you should be getting your hopes up. For one thing, she may already be interested in someone else."

"Who?"

"I'm not going down that road with you. I'm just saying that maybe you shouldn't—"

"Flash. Right?"

I didn't want to answer that.

He was suddenly morose.

"I *knew* it," he said.

Chapter 4

"Oh Adam was a kind man,
    And a wise man was he,
    He started asking questions,
    While on his mother's knee."

Anonymous folk song from
the early years of the Third Enlightenment

So that's how my life was, and—as far as I could see—how it was going to be from there on out.

After chapel, I had a whole day of classes. I continued to try to care about them, and sometimes I forgot my plight and fell into old habits: getting excited about the subject, or involved in a classroom debate.

But my world kept returning to the grey reality before me.

I didn't see Dolores until the next week, which surprised me when I thought about it. She had been so adamant that I expected she would hound me hourly.

I actually was hoping she would ask me about it, because

I'd finally decided what to say. I was going to tell her that I had changed my mind, that I knew Flash well enough to know he wasn't who she thought he was, that it would be a big mistake for her to get him interested. And then I was going to suggest that someone like Arthur would be a better choice.

When I pictured this conversation in my head, she always thanked me and took my advice. All I can say in my defense is that I was depressed at the time, and not thinking straight.

Finally I saw her in the refectory at lunch-time and decided to take the bull by the horns.

I dragged a chair next to her and sat down.

"Hey."

She looked up.

"Oh. Hi, Adam."

And she continued eating.

Apparently she wasn't going to help the conversation along.

I tried again.

"So, about Flash…"

"Flash?"

"You know. What you asked me to find out about whether he—"

"Oh. *That.* You can forget about that."

I was stunned. What could have happened in just a few days? Had Arthur managed to win her heart? Had she suddenly lost interest in boys altogether?

"Forget about it?"

She turned to me, her fork halfway to her mouth, and nodded.

"I don't need you to do that anymore."

She smiled.

"I'm sorry. I should have told you. But I've just been so, so *absorbed…*"

I was thoroughly lost.

"Absorbed?" I asked.

"Yes."

"Absorbed by?"

Flash put his tray down on the other side of her. He leaned forward and looked past Dolores at me.

"Hi Adam."

The look on her face told me all I needed to know.

So the two of them were a couple, now. Whatever that meant. I was off the hook. I didn't have to help it along, or try to stop it, and I supposed that my counseling sessions with Arthur would come to an end as soon he realized there was no hope left for him.

That left me with nothing to do but wallow in my own despair.

I wondered—had all my recent concern about others simply been a way to distract myself from my own bleak future?

And then I wondered about Flash. The last thing I'd have done in our mutual spiritual position would be to take on a girlfriend. For one thing I was too depressed to even think about anything like that. But beyond that I'd be worried that somehow my state would be, I don't know, *contagious* I suppose. That somehow I would drag her down with me.

But Flash was just going full steam ahead.

***

I WAS WRONG ABOUT ARTHUR. He came to see me that night in my room. I was studying for a test in hermeneutics and had finally got myself to actually focus on the material when he burst in my door. It was not the first time I'd wished the student rooms could be locked.

I knew the second he entered that the hermeneutics test was going to suffer. He sat on the edge of my bed and stared at his shoes.

"I don't know what to do," he mumbled.

I put my Bible down, and looked him over.

"About *what*, exactly?"

"You know. About Dolores."

"Dolores?"

"And Flash."

I puzzled over that for a moment. Then I took a stab at it.

"Look, Arthur. She didn't choose you. And you knew there wasn't much of a chance in the first place. So there's really only two options. You can forget the whole thing. Be sad for a while, sure. But realize that it's over, and move on. Or you can be patient and hold out hope that one day she'll grow tired of Flash and fall into your arms. I wouldn't recommend that, by the way. But either way there's not really anything for you to *do*."

He shook his head, then looked me in the eyes.

"I'm not an idiot, you know. I get that she's not going to be my girlfriend. I didn't need you to tell me that."

"Then what are you talking about?"

"I told you. Dolores and Flash. He's no good for her, Adam. He's not a nice person. One way or another he's going to cause her trouble."

I couldn't disagree.

He continued.

"I just feel like something has to be done. I—*we* have to figure out how to warn her, or stop him, or... or something."

He stared at his shoes again.

I was at a loss. He was right, of course, about the situation at least. But how to explain to the poor kid that it just had to play itself out, that nothing he or I could do would change a thing?

"Okay," I said. "Let's take those one at a time. If you or I tried to warn her, do you really think it would make any difference? Do you think, feeling the way she does at the moment, that she'd believe anything we had to say?"

He shook his head without looking up.

"And," I continued, "do you think we could stop *him*, even if we did try? What did you have in mind? Reasoning with him? Threatening him? Locking him in his room?"

This time he did look up.

"I know. I know. I just... I just don't want her to get hurt."

"That's the other thing. So he breaks her heart, or he's not nice to her. She'll live. She's in a pretty protected environment. Her father is the head of the school. How bad can it be?"

He looked at me like I was out of my mind.

I didn't blame him.

———

IT TURNED out the hermeneutics test was easy. I breezed through it without a sweat, in spite of the fact that I hadn't prepared well.

I made it through the next day without seeing Arthur or Dolores or Flash, no one questioned me about O.C.S., and I was only occasionally haunted by my permanently fallen state—though I never completely forgot about that.

Then came Thursday, and chapel, and the next sermon in Dr. Miller's series. This one was on the death of Saul. He dwelt heavily on the idea that Saul's disobedience had resulted not only in his own death, but in the death of his son as well.

This time I didn't have a promise to Dolores to distract me from the sermon, so I found myself paying attention, and wondering who else might pay for *my* sin.

That afternoon I spent my study period in the faculty lounge. It was a comfortable room, full of old overstuffed chairs and a couple of wooden tables. There was a fire-place on one wall—a real one, though I don't think it worked.

Pastor Dean taught introductory religion for the youngest students, and I graded their assignments for him. The faculty almost never used the faculty lounge in reality, so he had me do the work there. That day I had it entirely to myself.

Halfway through the period Pastor Dean dropped by to check on my progress, and took the opportunity to ask me about the O.C.S. matter.

"Has anyone asked you about it?"

"No sir, not at all."

"Good. I think you're in the clear if nothing's happened by now. You can forget about the whole thing."

"I will, sir," I lied.

I had no inclination to explain why exactly I would probably never forget about it.

He nodded.

"I'm really sorry I had to ask you to lie, Adam. And I'm very glad it never came to that. I'd have hated for you to be put in that position."

I didn't know what to say to that, so I changed the subject.

"I think I can get the rest of these done by the end of the period, sir."

He hadn't been gone more than ten minutes when I had another visitor.

The only thing keeping students out of the faculty lounge is the sign on the door, and the fear of getting caught. That's sufficient for most students. But Flash wasn't most students.

He closed the door behind him, and slipped into a chair.

I closed my Bible.

"You're not supposed to be in here."

He surveyed the room.

"So you get to work in here?"

"When I'm grading assignments."

He pointed to the wall behind me.

"What's that?"

I turned around and looked.

"It's called a dumb waiter. Back in the Dark Age, when the

seminary was first built, they used a kind of simple clockwork device to move food up here from the kitchen. There's ropes and wheels and stuff involved. But it hasn't been used since clockwork was outlawed."

He nodded.

"Oh yeah. Dolores told me about that."

"She did?"

"Yeah. You know that thing we talked about before, Kinde?"

"The unforgivable sin."

"Yeah," he said.

"You're still not supposed to be in here."

"It's gotten a bit more complicated."

That one threw me. Horrible, yes. Depressing, yes. But *complicated*? You'd either done it or you hadn't. It was pretty cut and dried.

"I don't understand. How can it be complicated?"

"Because," he said, "there's someone else involved now."

"Who?" I asked even though I could guess.

"Dolores."

"You've told *her* about it?"

"No. I haven't. It's not anything like that. It's just... well, I was feeling so lost, and she—she's so wonderful, Kinde. I can't tell you how great she is."

That did surprise me.

"So you really like her. And it's complicated because..."

"For lots of reasons. There's so many things..."

"Like?"

He thought about that.

"Well, one thing is: do I deserve it? I mean, after doing what I did?"

"Okay. I think I get that. What else?"

"Does she deserve to be around me? I'm doomed. Is it fair to connect her to all that?"

I nodded.

"Is that all?"

"Well, there's what you said. Should I tell her what I've done? Doesn't she deserve to know?"

I was in over my head at that point, and I knew it.

But Flash was on a roll.

"But," he continued, "if I tell her, what will she think of me? And how much should I tell her? If I tell her everything—I mean, you know, all the details—wouldn't that upset her? I just don't know what to—"

I interrupted.

"Look, Flash. I'd like to help. I really would. But this is way too complex for me."

"But what am I going to do?"

I considered, then had an inspiration.

"I think you should talk to Pastor Dean. Tell him everything and see what he says."

"But won't that get me in trouble?"

"I don't think so. Tell him you need to talk about something very personal, and get him to promise that it will be confidential before you start. He won't break a promise, I'm pretty sure of that."

"I don't know."

"Look. Could things really get worse? He might know something we don't. He might know how to deal with this kind of situation."

I had an ulterior motive, of course. I could almost count on Flash to tell me what Pastor Dean said, and I might learn something from that. Something that would apply to me.

BUT IT WASN'T to be. The next day was Friday, so there was no chapel service—just classes and studying. I didn't talk to Flash, or Dolores, or Arthur—though I did notice them all several times from a distance. Flash and Dolores would be holding hands or stealing a kiss. Arthur would be nearby, watching them and looking miserable.

I spent a lot of the time just brooding over my own doom. But you can't really sustain that. Not constantly. I'd get distracted—by a conversation, by my studies, by other things. And for a short time I would forget that my life was over.

Then I would remember, and for a brief moment I'd wish that I hadn't, that something big enough would happen to completely distract me for good, or at least for a very long time.

Be careful what you wish for.

I was in my room, after official lights out, doing logic problems for Mr. Smith's class. We were studying separation of cases and reductio, and I found both approaches to be fascinating, so I had put off going to bed.

I heard someone shouting in the hallway.

At first I ignored it, but the number of shouters multiplied, and I could hear people running down the hall, so I finally opened the door.

Everyone seemed to be gathering at the shower door at the top of the stairs, looking at something inside. As I approached someone pounded on the door to Pastor Dean's room, which was directly across from the showers. He opened the door, and several boys shouted something about a body.

He pushed his way through the crowd, and I followed close behind, so that he made way for me as well.

There, on the cold white tiles, lay Flash, the front of his shirt torn and soaked with blood.

GUILT AND INNOCENCE

Chapter 5

"The careful integration of a 'supernatural' worldview with empirical knowledge was reserved for the elite monastic technicians. The normal clergy were entrusted with just enough knowledge to give them the upper hand when dealing with lay people. This resulted, especially at the lower seminary levels, in a confusion between technology (officially called 'common miracles') and something approaching the idea of magic in earlier periods."

Lillian Trublood,
The Dynamics of Deception: Indoctrination Method and Practice During the Short Domination

PASTOR DEAN KNELT by the body and felt for a pulse, then turned to the nearest student.

"In my room, on my bed-stand, my Bible—bring it here. Hurry!"

He surveyed the room.

"Who found him?"

One of the younger students waved a tentative hand. He was ashen.

Pastor Dean pointed a finger at him.

"Stay here Ralph. Everyone else, back to your rooms."

He noticed me.

"Adam, you stay too. Guard the door. Check with me before letting anyone in."

The boy arrived back with the Bible. Pastor Dean grabbed it, polished the front surface, held it to Flash's lips, then looked for any mark of breath on it.

He shook his head, then made a circle on the surface and prayed for the healer, then for a word with the head of school. While he was waiting he addressed the students still standing there.

"I said back to your rooms! Now!"

He stood and waved a hand at me.

"Adam, move them out, then stand just inside."

I ushered the remaining students out the door, then took up my post, back to the door so I could watch.

One of the showers was slowly dripping. The sound echoed from the tiles on the walls, and a faint smell of soap permeated the air.

Pastor Dean put his Bible down and turned his attention to the young student.

"The head is on his way. While we're waiting, I'd like to hear your story, Ralph. Where were you before you came to the showers?"

"In my own room, sir."

"At the other end of the hall, yes?"

"Yes sir."

"So you came down the entire length of the hall. What did you see and hear on the way?"

"Nothing, sir. Nothing unusual, anyway."

"Was there anyone else in the hall?"

"No sir. It was empty."

"And the door to the showers. Was it open or closed when you arrived?"

"Closed, sir."

"So you opened it…"

"Yes sir, and I saw it—*him*, I mean sir—lying right there."

"Was there anyone else in this room?"

"Not that I saw, sir. I didn't think to look in the stalls."

"Of course not. Did you touch him at all?"

"No sir."

"You didn't try to wake him, or see if he needed help?"

"I was pretty sure he was dead, sir. From the way he looked."

Pastor Dean nodded.

"I understand. What did you do next, then?"

"I went into the hall, and I saw some of the older boys. I told them about the body."

"I see."

He put a hand on the boy's shoulder.

"Are you feeling all right?"

"I'm a little shook up, sir."

"I'm afraid I need you to stay until the head gets here. Do you think you can manage that?"

"I think so, sir."

"Why don't you take a seat on the bench there, while we wait?"

THE HEAD ARRIVED a few minutes after the healer. Dr. Miller was with him. I let them into the showers, closed the door behind them, and took up my post again, just inside the door.

The head surveyed the scene, then met Pastor Dean's gaze.

"Flash Andrews, right?"

"Yes."

"He's definitely dead, then?"

The healer nodded.

"When was he found?"

"In the last half hour," said Pastor Dean.

"And these boys?"

"Ralph, there, found the body. Adam is my student assistant. I've had him guarding the door after I sent everyone back to their rooms."

"So the entire floor knows about it?"

"The entire school will know by tomorrow."

"I see. Any idea what happened?"

"Ralph says he came for a shower, walked in the door, and saw the body where it is now. The hall was completely empty on his way here. I've kept him, in case you have other questions, but he's a bit shaken up."

"You've got his story already?"

"What there is."

"Let him go. I can talk to him later."

Dr. Miller, who had been silent until then, stepped forward.

"May *I* ask him a question?"

The head shrugged.

"Go ahead."

"What was your name, boy?"

"Ralph, sir."

"The chaplain asked you about what you saw already, Ralph?"

"He did, sir."

"And you told him everything?"

"I did sir."

"Now I want you to think carefully before you answer. When he was questioning you, did he say or do anything to make you think that you might be wrong about anything, or that perhaps that it would be better if some part of your story were left out?"

Ralph looked very puzzled, then shook his head.

"It's perfectly all right" Dr. Miller said. "You can tell us if he did."

Ralph looked from one to another of the adults, then shook his head again.

"No sir," he said. "I don't know what you mean, sir."

"Very well, then. You can go back to your room."

After Ralph had gone the head turned to Dr. Miller.

"What was that about?"

"Just being cautious. It's unfortunate that the first person to question the witness, and to do it without any other adults present, was himself a suspect."

"You're accusing Pastor Dean of murder?"

"Of course not. I'm just saying that he's definitely one of perhaps many suspects, until we get to the bottom of this. And unfortunately he was alone at the scene with the only witness we have for half an hour."

It was definitely not my place to say anything, but I couldn't help it.

"Not completely alone. I was here the whole time."

Miller gave a short, dismissive, laugh.

"Alone, except for his loyal student assistant. I believe he was your pastor as a child, Kinde?"

The head wasn't convinced.

"But why in the world should anyone suspect the chaplain?"

"You mean any more than they would suspect one of the boys, or another faculty member, or one of the staff? None of us wants to suspect anyone, of course. But look at the facts. The boy was stabbed to death; that much seems clear. Look at the front of his shirt. And there's another bloody tear in the back, so he was probably run right through."

He continued.

"So we're talking about someone strong enough to do that. And we're talking about someone with access to the showers in the late evening. That leaves us with the older students and the dorm supervisor—Pastor Dean. You don't want to believe he could do it. Neither do I, of course. But do we want to believe that it was one of the young man's fellow students?"

He took a deep breath before continuing.

"There's no weapon in sight. So it must be hidden somewhere, probably somewhere close by. No one saw the murderer come or go, so it's likely that he didn't travel far. Pastor Dean's room is conveniently located directly across the hallway. It would be a matter of a few steps for him to return there."

He looked from one of them to the other.

"We have to face the facts. I'm not saying he did it. I'm saying he's a suspect."

The head stared at him for a moment, then slowly shook his head.

"All of that's true. And it's still absurd. I've known Sam Dean for thirty years, and there's absolutely no possibility that he—"

Pastor Dean cut him off with a wave of his hand.

"He's right. There's no way around it. I'm a suspect. And I shut myself in here, with the body and the only witness, for at least twenty minutes. Luckily we have Ralph's word that I did nothing odd during that time, and the word of Adam as well."

He addressed Dr. Miller.

"And you're right. I *have* known Adam his whole life. And I've never met a more compulsively honest person, or a more observant one."

The head relented.

"Very well. So what do you propose, Dr. Miller?"

"We obviously need a rapid ecclesiastical inquiry. I suggest we contact Presbyter Brine."

PRESBYTER BRINE WAS A BEEFY MAN. His face was reddish, and dark. If I had to guess, I would guess that he drank too much. I had never seen him before, because he only taught in the seminary proper, unlike Dr. Miller who taught the rare class on our level.

We could hear his approach, a slow but steady '*thump, pause, thump, pause, thump*' as he made his way up the old wooden staircase. I opened the door and peered down the hall to make sure everyone was still in their rooms.

The hallway was empty, except for a few faces staring back at me from their own doorways.

When Dr. Brine appeared at the top of the stairs I held the door open for him, and he lumbered into the shower room. Once inside he stopped, breathing heavily for moment or two from the exertion of climbing the stairs. When he had recovered, he slowly circled the body once, then addressed the head.

"Unfortunate, all this. Perhaps you could, ahhh, provide some background?"

The head nodded toward Pastor Dean.

"The chaplain was the first faculty on the scene. His room is directly across the hall."

"Hmm." He turned his attention to Pastor Dean. "So you discovered the, the ahhh, body?"

"It was actually one of the younger students who gave the alarm. I came across to investigate the fuss, and ordered everyone but Ralph—the boy who found him—back to their rooms. I then got the boy's story, which appears to have been a mistake on my part."

"A mistake?"

"Yes. It appears that I'm a suspect, and that I shouldn't have spoken to a witness."

"You are, ahhh, a suspect?"

He exchanged a meaningful glance with Miller then, though I couldn't tell what the meaning was. The others didn't see it, because of the way everyone was standing, but I did.

Miller explained.

"The chaplain, and some of the older boys, seem to be the only ones with opportunity and the strength necessary. And the chaplain's room is just across the hall."

"Just across the hall?"

"Yes," Miller said. "And the weapon is missing."

"Missing." He looked at Pastor Dean. "That's very, ahhh, very unfortunate."

If I had been Pastor Dean I would have insisted that they search my room then and there. But for some reason he said nothing.

And no one else did either. They stood around the body in silence for what seemed like an endless time.

Finally, the head spoke.

"So, Dr. Brine, how do we proceed?"

"Yes. Well. Given the, ahhh, the circumstances, I wonder if Pastor Dean has any suggestions."

"I think," Pastor Dean replied, "that as a suspect it would be completely improper for me to make suggestions about the investigation."

"Then I suppose, as unfortunate as it seems, that I—that *we* —are forced, by the circumstances, you see, to request that you allow us to search your room."

PASTOR DEAN HELD the door to his room open for the others, and let them enter first. He told me to stand in the hall, and make sure all the students stayed in their rooms. I realized, when he said that, that I had been hoping to continue my eavesdropping. My disappointment seemed a bit unworthy, given that Flash was lying dead not ten feet away.

As it turned out, it didn't matter much because Pastor Dean left his door open as he followed the others in. Maybe it was to keep an eye on the hallway and the door to the showers, but I suspect he wanted me to witness the search of his room.

I stayed near the door just in case that was true.

Pastor Dean leaned against the wall, just inside, observing.

The head stood next to him, taking no part in the search.

Dr. Brine poked around the room, sticking a chubby finger into this and that, opening a drawer or two.

But Dr. Miller was thorough. He checked under the bed and the dressers and the desk. He examined every inch of the shelves in the closet. He opened boxes too small to contain a weapon, and he probed at the ceiling—I guess looking for the entrance to a crawl space. It took him a good half-hour, but in the end all he found was a tiny sculpture of a hand, held in the same ritual position you use to open your Bible or a locked door you have access to. It seemed to be made from the same material as our Bibles.

He showed it to Pastor Dean.

"Where did you come by this?"

"I found it earlier tonight, lying on the floor just outside my office."

"Do you know what it is?"

"I have no idea. Do you?"

"Oh yes. It is that rarest of treasures: the universal key. It will open any locked door in the world. More to the point, it will unlock any door in the seminary, allowing one to sneak around at will getting late night snacks from the refectory, snooping around your teacher's offices, pursuing whatever mischief a student's mind can conceive of."

"I didn't know such a thing existed."

Miller laughed.

"It doesn't. But generation after generation of students believe it does. Sometime ago, probably before either of us was born, an enterprising student in the Mind of God practicum put together the recipe for this little miracle, and made his exaggerated claims for it. It became a sort of legend, passed down from one class to the next, along with the recipe. Every couple of years someone manages to produce a copy and sneak it out of the workroom. Somehow word never gets around that it doesn't do anything at all."

"So it's meaningless."

"Probably. Where did you say you found it?"

"It was lying on the floor as I came out of my—oh, this may be important."

"How?"

"Not the... the *key* thing. But the reason I was in my office."

"And that was?"

"I was waiting for Flash."

Chapter 6

"Furthermore, several researchers have held, based upon rather cryptic comments attributed to Kinde in his later years, that it was during his early time in seminary that he first came to hear of Osseus."

Silas Redford,
The Real Adam Kinde: An Experiment in Biography

"You're saying that you, ahhh, had an appointment with the young man who was murdered?"

Pastor Dean frowned.

"Yes. I'm afraid I did. He never came, though. I finally gave up waiting for him and left for my room. That's when I found the 'key' on the floor."

"And this appointment," said Dr. Miller, "was for just before or, as far as we know, *at the same time* as his murder."

"I'm afraid that's so."

"What was this appointment about?" Miller asked.

"I don't actually know. He isn't in any of my classes at the moment, so he was seeing me in my capacity as chaplain. I presumed it was about some personal or spiritual problem."

"So you expect us to believe that you had an appointment to talk to this young man at approximately the time he was murdered, and that you have no idea what he wanted to talk about?"

Pastor Dean shrugged.

"It's what happened."

Dr. Brine folded his arms.

"I'm afraid that this, this *revelation* puts quite a different light on things. If you cannot bring yourself to, ahhh, to share with us the subject of this meeting, then we can only... only assume—"

I couldn't contain myself any longer.

"*I* know what the appointment was about," I blurted.

They all turned toward the door.

"You *do*?" said Pastor Dean.

"I was the one who suggested that he talk to you."

They looked at each other, then back to me.

"Well?" said Dr. Miller.

"It was a spiritual matter, sir. Flash came to me about it, but I didn't feel, I don't know, adequate to help him. So I suggested he talk to Pastor Dean."

"What was the nature of this 'spiritual matter'?"

"It was personal. I'd rather not say."

The head intervened.

"I can quite understand why you wouldn't want to betray a confidence, but under the circumstances..."

"That's exactly it," I said. "It would betray a confidence. He made me promise I would never tell anyone."

Pastor Dean decided to help me out.

"Could you answer some *general* questions about his concern without telling us exactly what it was?"

"What kind of questions?"

"Was there anything about his problem that could have had anything at all to do with his murder? Had he done anything, for example, that might cause someone to be upset or angry with him?"

I thought immediately of Arthur, and then of Dolores. But he would never have told Arthur about his fantasies, and he hadn't told Dolores yet, because that was exactly what he had wanted to talk to Pastor Dean about.

I swallowed.

"No. It was nothing like that. It had more to do with his... his *prayer* life."

I hoped that would kill their interest.

Pastor Dean turned toward the others and waited.

Luckily, the head decided to take charge.

"I think we can leave it at that for the moment, Adam. But we may need to come back to you later on this point."

Dr. Miller was clearly not happy with that, and I couldn't tell what Dr. Brine was thinking, but apparently I was off the hook for the moment.

WHILE THE HEALER and his staff removed the body, Dr. Miller searched all of the stalls in the shower room for the weapon or any other clue. The head and Dr. Brine supervised the whole process.

I stayed with Pastor Dean in his room. I had something I wanted to ask him.

"There's something I don't understand."

"What's that?"

"You knew there was no evidence against you in your room, so why didn't you *suggest* they search it?"

He looked at me with interest.

"Shut the door."

When I had done that, he continued.

"There were several reasons I didn't offer. The least important one was sheer perversity. Dr. Miller and Dr. Brine obviously wanted me to, and just between you and me I don't care much for either one of them."

He glanced at the door.

"A more pragmatic reason was the effect it would have. If I had suggested a search that found nothing, they could easily argue that I only suggested it because I had hidden the evidence elsewhere."

I nodded.

"The results of a search *they* insisted on," I said, "would be more believable than the results of a search suggested by a suspect."

"Exactly. But there's more to it than that. Miller doesn't like me much to begin with, but I suspect that that his obvious enthusiasm to pin this murder on me has to do with that matter I asked you to lie about."

I was shocked.

"He'd do that?"

"He might. There's more at stake than I can tell you about."

"But *murder*, sir?"

"It won't be the death penalty. Remember, I'm a member of the clergy and the murder happened on seminary property, so it's entirely an ecclesiastical matter. I'm not going to face the rod for this. The worst that can happen is that I'll be sent to a hermitage."

"In prison for life."

"Or dedicated to contemplation for the rest of my life, depending on how you look at it."

"And it's my fault. For repeating what I heard in front of him."

I took a deep breath.

"I need to tell you something else I did."

He glances at the door again.

"Make it quick."

"I didn't talk to anyone about it, but I *did* try to look it up again. Mr. Matthews gave us permissions to do a little research in the Dark Age archives, and I used it to do a search. You don't think Dr. Miller could have found out?"

"I don't know. What did you find?"

"A whole list of possibilities, but none of them made any sense. Obsessive Compulsive Syndrome, Officer Candidate School, Outer something..."

"I don't understand. Where did you look?"

"I just did a search on the initials O.C.S., and—"

He actually laughed.

"That's what you heard? O period, C period, S period?"

I nodded.

He stared at me in silence for a moment, then appeared to make up his mind about something.

"They'll be back any moment, so listen carefully. You misheard what was said. It wasn't the three initials O.C.S. It was a name—Osseus. A name I want you to forget you ever heard, except for two things: If you ever hear that name again, stay clear of it. Don't get curious, and *don't* try to find out more. And, if you *do* get questioned, tell them all about the initials, confess your illegal search—they'll be sure to confirm it, and when they do they'll lose all interest in you. That will protect you far better than all the lies I suggested before. If they think that's all you heard, they'll leave you completely alone."

"But what about *you*, sir?"

Before he could answer Dr. Brine opened the door. His eyes

moved from Pastor Dean to me and back again before he held up a bible.

"You left it on the bench, Pastor. I'll be confiscating it until this matter is settled."

———

THAT WAS the last chance I had to talk to Pastor Dean. Dr. Brine confined him to his room and ordered him not to talk to anyone until the inquiry.

He then asked me to clean the shower room floor where the body had been. Pastor Dean objected, saying I had done enough, and a friend of mine had just died, but I said I didn't mind. And I didn't. I looked at it as my last chance to do something for Flash. That may not make a lot of sense, but it was how I felt.

And actually there wasn't much to clean up, which surprised me.

I got to thinking about it, and remembered Mr. Smith's logic exercises. I applied separation of cases to the lack of blood, and suddenly felt a lot better. It didn't make any sense that the murderer would have cleaned up the blood, so the murder must have happened somewhere else, and the body had been moved. That's where separation of cases came in:

Separation of Cases: Either Pastor Dean moved the body or he didn't.

Case 1: If Pastor Dean *didn't* move the body, presumably the murderer did, to avoid suspicions the original location would raise. Conclusion: Pastor Dean isn't the murderer.

Case 2: If Pastor Dean *did* move the body (which I very much doubted) he moved it to a place that *caused* him to be suspected. So he must have moved it to protect someone *else*. Conclusion: Pastor Dean isn't the murderer.

In either case Pastor Dean was innocent.

So I felt a lot better.

And then I realized *why* it made me feel so much better, and I felt a lot worse.

Because the truth was that all of Pastor Dean's talk about this mysterious Osseus, his talk about what was at stake, and his apparent willingness to accept the punishment if he could just keep me out of it all—all of that had made me worry, just a little bit, whether he really was innocent.

I was ashamed of myself for that.

But the absence of blood on the floor and the methods from logic class made it absolutely clear to me that Pastor Dean couldn't be the killer.

It also made me determined to find out who was.

***

IT WAS LATE, but no one was going to be sleeping soon, after the excitement of Flash's murder. And with Pastor Dean confined to his room, there was no authority to force lights out.

I had two ideas about where to start. The first was Flash's room. I might find something there that would give me something to go on. The second idea made me nervous, so I decided to put it off.

When I approached Flash's room, the door was already open.

I slowed down and listened. There were voices inside.

I stopped just before reaching the door and listened harder. It was Dr. Miller and Dr. "Ahhh" Brine.

"You're absolutely certain that he used the, ahhh, the *name*? It wouldn't do to use measures, *extreme* measures that is, on a false suspicion."

"I heard the boy myself. Clear as day."

"And you're sure Dean knew what he was talking about?"

"He shut him up about it immediately, and changed the

subject. I don't think there can be much doubt. Perhaps we should interrogate young Kinde."

"No. That would be, ahhh, imprudent. We would just make the boy more curious. If he was, was *asking*, it means he didn't know. And Dean is no fool. He wouldn't risk getting a student involved."

"So should we do a little tampering, or..."

"I don't, don't think, you know, that it would be wise. This is, as you say, a... a golden opportunity to deal with the Pastor Dean problem, if it is a problem, but we must be, ahhh, careful not to leave any loopholes, if you follow me."

"Less actual evidence is safer than creating evidence that might backfire."

"Precisely."

"You're probably right. Still..."

"The actual weapon does exist, you know. Probably on this floor somewhere, which would still give him access."

I decided to follow up on my second idea instead. I walked past the door without turning my head and continued down the hall.

But they had seen me.

"Mr., ahhh, Mr. Kinde! Would you step in here for a moment?"

I came back to the doorway, where I stopped and waited.

The room was a mess. The mattress was pulled off the bed, drawers had been pulled out of the desk and the contents dumped out. Clothes were scattered all over. Dr. Miller was crouched down, searching through a dresser drawer on the floor. He paused and looked up.

"Have you been here before us, Kinde?"

"No sir. I've been cleaning up the shower room floor."

"I meant earlier. Perhaps before the alarm was sounded?"

"No sir."

He waved his hand at the general disarray.

"Well, someone has."

"You found it like this, sir?"

He gave one of his sardonic chuckles.

"You thought *we* did this?"

"No sir. That is, I didn't actually think about it one way or the other, sir."

On the wall, above the head of the bed, hung an ornate sword in its scabbard. Dr. Miller saw me staring at it.

"We've noticed it, if you're wondering. It's not the weapon."

"It's not, sir?"

"It's a showpiece, not even sharp enough to cut butter."

I nodded.

"Then I suppose they all are."

That got his attention. He forgot the drawer and stood up.

"What do you mean?"

"Flash and his friends all have one hanging in their rooms. It was a sort of club or something. They call themselves 'The Order of the Sword'."

"So there are more of these, in other rooms. How many?"

"I don't know for sure. Maybe four or five."

"And the names of the other members of this club?"

I gave them a list, but I left one name out.

Chapter 7

I LEFT that one name off the list because he was my second idea. I wanted a chance to get to him before they did.

Eddie White's door was also standing open, and he was sitting at his desk inside. He looked up when I knocked on the door jamb.

"Hey, Kinde. Come on in."

His room smelled of dirty socks.

"Hi Eddie."

He looked me over.

"I can't get my mind around it. Flash. Murdered." He shook his head. "So you've been in the thick of it all."

"I have."

"Do they know who did it?"

"They suspect Pastor Dean, but only because the shower is right across from his room. He didn't do it."

Eddie got a funny look in his eyes.

"I wouldn't be too sure of that."

"What do you mean?"

"Flash knew something—something *incriminating* about your wonderful pastor friend."

A voice came from the doorway.

"And what was that?"

It was Dr. Miller. He glanced from Eddie to the sword on his wall, then back to me.

"I see you left a name off the 'Order of the Sword' list, Kinde."

"Sorry, sir," I said. "I knew Eddie was his friend. I didn't know he was a member of that group."

He clearly didn't believe me. He turned his attention back to Eddie.

"What did Flash know about Pastor Dean?"

Eddie sat up straighter.

"He was having an affair, sir, with another teacher's wife."

"Which one?"

"I don't know, sir. Flash didn't say."

Miller nodded, then stepped across the room and took the sword out of its scabbard. He touched an edge.

"You keep this razor-sharp. Why?"

Eddie shrugged.

"I don't know sir, really. I never actually use it for anything."

"I'm going to have to take this with me, as possible evidence."

He put it back in the scabbard, stuck the scabbard under his arm, gave me a final hostile glance, and left the room. Just outside the door he paused and fired one last question at Eddie.

"Where were you this evening? Between dinner and the time the body was found?"

Eddie's eyes widened.

I was with some friends, sir, in the student lounge, until lights out. You can ask anyone."

Miller thought about that.

"Then someone could have come into your room, and you wouldn't have known?"

"No sir. I mean, yes sir. I wouldn't have known, sir."

Miller smiled to himself.

"Come to my office before breakfast tomorrow morning, Eddie."

Eddie got up and stood in the doorway, watching him go down the hall. After a moment he closed the door and stared at me.

"So you didn't give up my name to him. I may have misjudged you, Kinde."

"This affair thing," I said. "Are you sure Flash was talking about Pastor Dean?"

"Yeah. No question." He changed the subject. "You were there when they were going over everything—the, um, the body and all?"

"They had me guarding the door."

"Did they *find* anything? In his pockets or anything?"

"Not that I remember. What kind of thing?"

"A kind of sculpture. Small. Shaped like a hand. He borrowed it from me yesterday, and it wasn't in his room after..."

So it was Eddie who had searched Flash's room. I decided to play dumb.

"What was it for?"

"It was a key. A way to open a door you don't have access to. Don't tell anyone about this, okay?"

"Did he say which door he wanted to open with it?"

"He didn't say anyplace special. We'd talked about a lot of places we could use it. The kitchen, teachers' offices, the practicum workroom…"

I phrased my answer carefully.

"There was nothing like that in his pockets."

IT WAS LATE, and the hall was empty as I headed back to my room. I was pretty close to giving up. Not because I didn't want to know, and not because the whole thing looked hopeless—which it did. It was because the more I tried to help Pastor Dean the worse it looked for him.

If I'd just kept my nose out of it all I'd have never told Dr. Miller about the swords, and Eddie would never have said anything about Pastor Dean having an affair (which I still didn't believe), and that sword would still be hanging on Eddie's wall.

All I was doing was making it worse.

At least Dr. Miller didn't hear what Eddie had said about the little hand. It was obviously the "universal key" that was found in Pastor Dean's room. If they found out that Flash had had it before he was killed it would be another nail in Pastor Dean's coffin.

I didn't want to think about that.

But I couldn't help wondering why Flash had borrowed it. There was no point in borrowing it unless he thought it was real. So he must have wanted to use it to unlock a door. Which door? The refectory kitchen, the workroom, or a teacher's office? Which teacher? Pastor Dean?

I really didn't want to think about that, either.

And was that place, wherever it was, the real scene of the murder? Maybe he got caught doing whatever it was he was doing, and the person who caught him killed him.

That gave me another idea.

People didn't generally carry large knives around. If I was right—if he was killed in the room he was sneaking into, then it had to be a room with large knives in it.

The kitchen had large knives. I'd never been in the workroom, but it might have some as well. I didn't remember any knives in Pastor Dean's office.

I paused outside my door. There was still no one in sight, and the stairs were just down at the end of the hall.

The "key" didn't work, if Dr. Miller was telling the truth. So once Flash got there he would have had to break in some other way. It might still be open.

I kept right on walking, to the end of the hall and down the stairs.

It wasn't unheard of for students to sneak down at night, but it didn't happen often. Flash had apparently done it, or at least planned to. But I wasn't one of those students. I tended to follow the rules. So this was my first time wandering the seminary halls at night.

It was spooky. The lights were very low in the hallways, and my footsteps echoed as I walked. I kept thinking I heard another set of footsteps behind me, but every time I stopped it was silent.

But I still had the feeling I was being followed.

I decided to check Pastor Dean's office last, if at all. The workroom was clear at the other end of the building, so I tried the kitchen first. It was a floor lower than the chapel and the faculty lounge, so I passed Pastor Dean's office on the way to the stairs.

The kitchen was always locked. Only the people working there were allowed in. But the refectory was never locked. It was nothing but tables and chairs, so what would be the point?

It was, however, dark. I used a chair to prop the door open so a little light could come in from the hallway. I made my way across the room, only bumping into a table once or twice. The door to the kitchen was shut. And it was still locked.

So Dr. Miller was right. The key didn't work. If this was where Flash was going he must have found another way in. I felt my way along the wall to the counter which stuck out below the serving window. Just as I felt the edge, I thought I saw something move in the hall. I stopped, and watched the doorway for what seemed like forever, but nothing appeared.

The serving window had a solid shutter which lowered from inside the kitchen. I pushed at it, and pried a little as well, but it didn't move. I slid my hand along the top of the counter as I walked to the opposite end, and just before I got there I felt a hole. I recognized it as the opening we dumped the garbage into when we bussed our dishes.

That gave me an idea. The can we dumped the garbage into was directly below the hole, and I remembered that there was a door just under the counter for access to the can. There might be a door on the other side, for access from the kitchen.

I felt under the counter and found the door. It opened easily. I pulled the can out with some effort, and crawled into the space it left. I felt along the wall at the back. I found another door.

I pushed on it. It didn't give. I found an edge, and pried at that. Nothing.

I backed out of the cramped space and slid the garbage can back into place, closed the door in front of it, and stood up.

Just as I did I caught another movement out of the corner of my eye—or at least thought I did. But once again, it was gone when I looked at the doorway.

I felt my way to the end of the counter, gave a half-hearted push and tug at the shutter there, and decided the kitchen was not going to yield any secrets. I made my way back across the room to the hallway.

When I got to the door, I peeked around the corner—half expecting to see my phantom follower—but there was no one there.

THE WORKROOM WAS at the far end of the building, on the lowest level. You had to go down a narrow flight of stairs, probably not intended for general use. At the bottom was a short hallway with only two doors.

One door led into the basement storage areas. I knew that because I had helped bring flats and props up for school plays when I'd served on stage crew.

The other door led to the workroom.

It was locked, and it showed no signs of anyone trying to force it open. This was a lot simpler than the kitchen. It was, as far as I knew, the only door to the workroom.

That left Pastor Dean's office, unless I could think of some other possibility.

I climbed the stairs again, trying hard to think of some other place to try. I swung the stairway door open at the top, and stopped dead in my tracks.

Someone had just disappeared around the corner down the hall. I was sure of it.

I stood perfectly still, listening.

Nothing. Not a sound.

Whoever it was, he was now between me and my room, so there wasn't much I could do about it.

I still hadn't thought of any new places to look, so I reluctantly headed upstairs to Pastor Dean's office. But at the top of the stairs I passed the faculty lounge, and had a sudden thought.

I remembered Flash asking about the dumb waiter. And I remembered that the dumb waiter connected to the kitchen.

I stepped through the doorway.

I had to prop the door open again, like I had in the refectory, to let some light in from the hall. It was easier crossing the room though—it was smaller and had less furniture.

At first glance, the dumb waiter didn't look like anyone had messed with it. The door had a little wooden knob on one side. I pulled on it, and the hinges complained a bit as it creaked open.

Inside was a wooden box, set back a bit from the door, and two ropes, one on each side. It was just barely large enough that I could imagine Flash cramming himself into it. But could he have moved freely enough to operate the thing once he was inside?

I tugged on one of the ropes experimentally, and nothing happened. I tugged on the other one and the box moved about an inch downward, then stuck.

I pulled harder.

It wouldn't budge.

I tried the other rope again.

It still wouldn't budge.

I pushed the box to one side while pulling and it popped back up to its original position.

I realized that I was just procrastinating, putting off the moment I was dreading. That thing probably hadn't worked in ages, and even if it had I couldn't see how Flash could have managed to control it while stuck inside. In all probability the door at the kitchen end had been walled up or nailed shut long ago.

I closed the door to the thing and left the lounge. There was no sign of my follower in the hallway. I headed for Pastor Dean's office.

I shouldn't have worried so much.

His office was no different from the workroom. A single door, no sign of anyone trying to get in. So my expedition seemed to be a failure. It was time to throw in the towel and return to my room. I breathed a sigh of relief.

But my very next thought brought a sinking feeling with it, in the pit of my stomach. Pastor Dean was the chaplain.

So his office was next door to the chapel.

It didn't bear thinking about.

But I couldn't leave it alone. I entered the chapel by the door at the front, the one he used when coming from his office. There was a wedge on the floor there, to hold the door open, so I didn't have to move any furniture this time.

I crossed to the altar, stepped onto the platform, and went directly to the center of the back wall. I peered into the case that held the lamp and the sword, but there wasn't enough light to see.

I peered closer, and suddenly there was even less light.

Someone was standing in the doorway.

Chapter 8

"The result of this division in the justice system was that the clergy, while immune from secular punishments, were firmly under the thumb of the church hierarchy while at the same time their crimes were never heard of by the general public. A pastor's transgressions were kept secret, and punishment was mild, unless, of course, his behavior threatened the religious establishment."

Joyce Matisse,
Crime and Punishment During the Short Domination.

HE WAS SILHOUETTED against the dim light of the hallway, so I couldn't see who it was at first. But then he spoke.

"Let me help you out."

It was Dr. Miller. He turned to the light panel by the door and gestured a quick circle. The chapel was flooded with light.

"There," he said. "That's better. Can you see it now?"

"See what?"

He chuckled.

"You've been a great help in this matter, Kinde. Let's see if you've discovered anything important."

He stepped up beside me and peered into the case.

"Yes. I believe you have. Most of the blood has been wiped away, but there's still a little bit—high on the blade, up by the hilt. Well done!"

"It doesn't prove anything."

"Well, that's open to debate. I think we'll leave that right where it is until tomorrow. In the meantime..."

He turned his attention to the floor in front of the case. It was tile, and he gave his attention to the cracks between the tiles.

"Yes," he said. "Just here. He got most of it cleaned up, but not all. He was probably rushed by circumstances."

He beamed at me.

"You've been so much help tonight that I think I'll overlook the fact that you've been wandering about after lights out. Go to bed. I won't report you."

I slunk back to my room.

THE INQUIRY WAS SCHEDULED IMMEDIATELY after breakfast the next morning. It was to be held in the chapel. The only people required to attend were those directly involved. That included me, because I had been designated a witness.

But it was a Saturday, which meant no classes were being held, and interest in Flash's death was high, so the place was filling up by the time I got there. Since it wasn't a formal chapel, the students were sitting wherever they pleased, and the front seats were filling up first.

I came in from the back out of force of habit. I was in a

kind of daze from lack of sleep and the excitement of the previous evening, so I found myself staring at the floor as I came in. It was made up of tiny square stone tiles in various colors and patterns, some stamped with a simple design. I'd noticed it a thousand times before. The design was one of those things—like the hymn and scripture boards or the window where students could see Dr. Thomas walking on water—that bugged me. I always wanted to know what it meant.

This morning something about it seemed particularly significant to me. I couldn't quite put my finger on what it was, though.

The altar had been removed from the front of the platform, and in its place was an ornate chair. I recognized it as a throne from one of the recent school plays.

On the chapel floor, between the pews and the platform was a curved table, shaped like a giant "C" facing the throne. Dr. Miller sat at the right end. Eddie White sat next to him, and young Ralph Simmons, who had found the body, sat next to Eddie. Pastor Dean sat on the left end, with Dr. Thomas beside him. The middle had several empty chairs.

I'd been told at breakfast that as a witness I was part of the inquiry, so I took the seat next to Dr. Thomas—as far from Dr. Miller as I could get.

I assumed that Dr. Brine would be sitting on the throne and running the inquiry. While we were waiting for him to arrive, students kept drifting in and filling the seats. There was no worship music, so people were chatting in the pews. To my surprise I saw Dolores and Arthur sitting together in the front row. She was looking very upset, and gripping his hand. She didn't seem to be aware of anything going on around her.

Finally, Dr. Brine arrived, in his full doctoral robes, followed by his guardian angel. He took his place on the throne and waited as the room became quiet. The angel stood just behind to the left of the throne. Once there was silence, Dr. Brine spoke.

"We are here today to inquire into... ahhh... *questions* which have arisen in connection with... with recent unfortunate events.

"It is important that all involved understand that this is *not* a civil hearing. We are here as a... a community of clergy, and our purpose is not punishment, as those in the society outside these walls would seek, but rather... ahhh... rather to decide on the best course forward for all, and specifically the best course forward for Pastor Dean, whose role in these matters we are here to determine.

"The first step, then, is to understand the facts of the situation. And that is where we will begin. For that purpose, Dr. Miller will pursue the inquiry on behalf of the church, and Dr. Thomas, the head of school, will raise questions on behalf of Pastor Dean.

"Dr. Miller, will you begin please?"

Dr. Miller rose from his seat and surveyed the audience before speaking.

"As this community probably knows by now, Flash Andrews was found murdered last night. We are here to look into questions surrounding that murder. Questions which bear on Pastor Dean's future in the church."

He paused, then continued.

"Ralph Simmons, you were the one who discovered the body?"

Ralph nodded.

"You'll need to answer us with words, boy. And loud enough for all to hear."

"Yes sir. I discovered it, sir."

"And when did you discover it?"

"After lights out, sir. I hadn't showered, and I was still sweaty from games in the afternoon. I was having trouble sleeping, so I just thought if I—"

Dr. Miller cut him off.

"All we're concerned with here is the murder. Where did you find the body?"

"In the shower room, sir."

"And did you see, or hear, anyone else on your way to the shower room?"

"No sir."

"No other students about?"

"No sir."

"Whose room is closest to the shower room?"

Ralph looked at Pastor Dean, but said nothing.

Dr. Miller snapped at him.

"Ralph!"

The boy jumped in his seat.

"Whose room is closest?"

"Pastor Dean's, sir."

"Thank you."

He now turned his attention to Eddie White, and held out the universal key.

"Mister White. Do you recognize this object?"

"Yes sir."

"Would you tell us what it is, please?"

Eddie squirmed in his chair.

"It's, well, it's *supposed* to be a universal key."

"And what is a universal key supposed to do?"

"It's supposed to open any door you want to open."

"And this key belongs to you?"

"Yes sir."

"I won't ask you where you got it, because it doesn't work. But *you* thought it would work, didn't you?"

"I did, sir."

"And Flash thought it would work as well?"

"Yes sir."

"And you loaned it to him before he was murdered?"

"Yes sir. I did."

Dr. Miller let that sink in, then changed the subject.

"Did Flash ever mention Pastor Dean to you in the days before he died?"

The head interrupted, without standing.

"Excuse me. I have a question for Eddie about this 'key'. *When* did you lend the key to Flash, Eddie?"

"A couple of days ago. I think it was Thursday, after chapel."

"Thank you."

He nodded to Dr. Miller, who continued.

"Did Flash ever mention Pastor Dean to you?"

"Yes. About a week ago."

"And what did he say?"

"He told me that Pastor Dean was having an affair with the wife of another faculty member."

A gasp went through the room.

"Did he say which one?"

"No. He just said that he had seen them together."

"Thank you."

He did another one of his dramatic pauses, took a deep breath, and turned his attention to me.

"MR. KINDE. When did you first become aware of Flash's death?"

"I heard the commotion outside my room and went down to the showers to see what it was about."

"Was Pastor Dean there when you arrived?"

"He came out of his room just as I got there."

"And when he sent the others away, he asked you to stay and guard the door?"

"That's right."

"So you had a good look at the body."

"I suppose."

"What was the wound like?"

"He had blood on his shirt. Front and back."

"Like he had been stabbed through, with a long blade?"

"Yes."

"And you were still there, after Dr. Brine and I arrived, when we searched Pastor Dean's room?"

"Yes."

"And what did we find in his room?"

I glanced at Pastor Dean, who nodded for me to answer.

I mumbled, "The key."

"Speak up!"

"The key."

He held it up for all to see.

"This key?"

"Yes."

"And after that you didn't go directly to bed, did you?"

"No. I didn't."

"You actually wandered the seminary for some time, searching for something."

"Yes."

"And what were you searching for?"

I saw an opportunity.

"I knew that Pastor Dean didn't do it."

"Please confine yourself to answering the question. What were you searching for?"

"I *am* answering the question. There was no blood on the floor of the shower. So—"

"Mr. Kinde." Dr. Brine interrupted me. "Please simply answer the question Dr. Miller asked."

"I was trying to find out where Flash had been killed."

The head intervened again.

"I would like to hear Adam's reasoning on this matter. How did you know Pastor Dean was innocent?"

"There wasn't any blood under Flash's body, so it must have been moved there from somewhere else. But the murderer wouldn't move it right next door to his own room. That would be stupid."

What had sounded so obvious to me the night before sounded pretty weak in the middle of a formal inquiry.

I added lamely, "You know, separation of cases." But it made no sense in the context.

Dr. Miller smiled.

"So you were convinced that if you found the real location of the murder, it would tell you who the murderer was?"

"I just thought... I guess so." This wasn't going well.

"And you found that location, didn't you?"

"Yes."

"Speak up, please."

"Yes."

"And where was it?"

"Here."

"Here. In the chapel, not twenty feet from Pastor Dean's office?"

"Yes."

"There was blood on the floor, in the cracks between the tiles?"

"Yes."

"And the weapon still had blood on it?"

"Yes."

"And where was the weapon?"

"In the case."

"It was the *Sword of the Word*, correct?"

There was another gasp from the room.

Chapter 9

"Thus, the various stories which give him a larger role than that of a witness in the inquiry concerning the chaplain are almost certainly apocryphal."

Silas Redford,
The Real Adam Kinde: An Experiment in Biography

WHEN DR. MILLER began to question Pastor Dean, and I realized my own testimony was over, I fell back into a kind of trance. I was still exhausted from the lack of sleep, but I think it was mostly just the letdown from being on the spot like that.

I found my mind wandering back to the symbol on the stones in the chapel floor, trying to figure out what had seemed so significant about it. Something different than before. But I couldn't place it.

After a while I forced my attention back to the inquiry. Dr. Miller was speaking.

"...exactly was this appointment Flash made with you?"

Pastor Dean was answering calmly, with a steady voice.

"After dinner, the night he was killed," said Pastor Dean.

"And *where* were you planning to meet?"

"In my office."

"Which is right next to this chapel?"

"It is." He didn't seem the least bit frightened.

I couldn't stay focused. I think I was half asleep. I kept seeing that symbol in my head, and wondering why it was important. And then wondering why things like that always bugged me. The head walking on water...

I heard my name mentioned and forced my attention back to the questioning again.

"...heard Mr. Kinde testify to finding the weapon, still bloodstained, here in the chapel?"

"I did."

"And has it occurred to you to ask yourself why it is still there, in the case?"

For the first time a hint of worry crept into Pastor Dean's voice.

"What do you mean?"

"Why, Pastor Dean, do you think it is that we have not removed this important piece of evidence for safe keeping?"

As he recognized the significance of that question I saw fear in his eyes for the first time.

"Because you... you *can't*."

"And would you please explain *why* we can't?"

"Because as chaplain, I'm the only one with access."

"So you are the only one who could open the cabinet? The only one who could take the sword out, or put it back?"

Now he looked confused, and troubled.

"Yes... *Yes!* Except I *didn't!*"

For the third time that day there was a gasp in the room,

and then Dr. Brine announced that we would reconvene after lunch.

I stayed in my seat, shocked and discouraged and exhausted. The head and Pastor Dean rose and walked around me, passing Dolores and Arthur on the way to the exit. Arthur was trying to get Dolores to stand. He probably thought she should eat something. But she was in an even deeper stupor than I was.

I stared at them, my mind wandering back to that symbol on the floor, and the other things that bugged me, the window looking over the lake, the hymn and scripture boards, the dumb waiter in the faculty lounge...

Why was I thinking about the dumb waiter? That wasn't one of the things that bugged me.

I shook my head to clear the cobwebs and wake myself up. There was an idea there. I knew it. I pictured that symbol again. I thought about the dumb waiter and Flash. I looked at the hymn and scripture boards.

Something shifted.

Suddenly I thought I knew everything. Well, *almost* everything.

And then I realized I had a very difficult task ahead of me.

I DIDN'T HAVE time to eat lunch. I headed back to the student rooms, past the showers and down the hallway—past my own room to his.

It was cleaner and neater than most. I don't know if that made it any easier to search. It took me some time, but I found it, eventually, crammed under the bed.

The thing that had bugged me about those symbols on the floor was simply that I could see them. I had seen the same symbols all over the floor of the chapel, every time I'd been in the room, but I'd never seen them *there*, at the entrance, because they had always been covered by an old threadbare rug.

But not this morning.

Because that rug had been used to move Flash's body.

And now I had found it.

I pulled it out and examined it. Blood. Not a lot, but enough to make it clear that I was right—at least about this part.

The next part was going to be tricky. I couldn't tell the head everything for fear he would refuse to cooperate. I took the rug back to my own room and wrapped it in the blanket from my bed, so I could carry it to the chapel without anyone seeing what I had.

There was no one there, so I stashed it under the table by my seat and waited.

THEY ALL CAME in together so I didn't have a chance to explain things to the head in any detail. I was actually glad of that. Too much explanation could have ruined everything.

I just told him I had found some new evidence and that I thought it would help Pastor Dean. He raised his eyebrows in surprise, but before he could ask me about it Dr. Brine called us to order.

He requested that Dr. Miller summarize the morning's findings and said we would hear anything the head wanted to add after that.

Dr. Miller laid it on thick. According to him, the evidence painted an obvious picture. Flash had witnessed Pastor Dean having an affair with the wife of a fellow faculty member and had made an appointment in order to blackmail him—probably for some favor in his capacity as chaplain. Pastor Dean had met him in the chapel, killed him with the sword, cleaned up the mess, and moved the body to the shower in order to add the entire student body to the list of suspects.

In the process he had inadvertently ended up with the key, which he hadn't had time to hide before his room was searched.

As he was the only person in the school who had access to the cabinet, he was the only one who could have killed Flash.

After he was finished he sat down, and Dr. Brine asked if the head had anything to add. I held my breath, hoping that he would trust me enough to ask me about my evidence.

He clearly took his time thinking about it, but finally he did.

"I understand, Adam, that you have uncovered some new evidence during the lunch break."

I reached down and pulled out the rug. I placed it on the table, and pulled back my blanket so everyone could see what it was.

"This is the rug that's normally on the floor, just at the back entrance to the chapel. I found it in the boys' dormitory. It has blood on it, so it was probably used to move Flash's body."

"So now we know," Dr. Miller said, "how Pastor Dean transported the poor young man's remains to the shower room."

"No sir."

He didn't like that.

"Do you need to be reminded that you are here to answer our questions, *not* to instruct us?"

But the head intervened.

"I'd like to hear what he has to say."

He turned to me.

"Why doesn't this point just as much to Pastor Dean as the previous evidence, Adam?"

"Because, sir, I found it under the bed of a student. A student whose room is at the far end of the hall from the showers."

"Does this student have a name?"

"Arthur."

The head sat up straighter in surprise, and cast a glance at his daughter in the front pew.

"Arthur George?"

"Yes sir."

He motioned for Arthur to join us.

"Come up here, Arthur, and take a seat at the table."

Arthur looked terrified. He stood and forcibly pulled his hand from Dolores's grip. When he was seated, the head spoke again.

"How did this rug end up under your bed?"

"I put it there, sir."

"And why did you have it in the first place?"

"I... I used it to move the... to move Flash, sir."

"*You* moved the body?"

"Yes sir. I..." He wet his lips. "I killed him sir."

DR. MILLER EXPLODED. "I don't know who put you up to this, boy, but you can't reasonably expect us to believe it!"

"We may or may not believe it," said the head, "but I would like to hear Arthur's story."

He looked at Arthur and waited.

"Well," Arthur said, "I... I was very upset about Flash and... and your daughter, sir. I didn't think he was good for her. So I followed them, and when I saw them kissing in the chapel, I just got angry. So I killed him."

He glanced around the table before continuing.

"Then I went out to a supply closet in the hall and found some rags, and I got the carpet from the back of the chapel, and I rolled him onto the carpet and scrubbed the floor and dragged him all the way to the stairs.

"It was hard getting him up the stairs, but I kind of folded the carpet around him and held it by the edges, and then I could lift him that way, one step at a time."

He stopped, and looked down at his hands.

The room was dead silent.

I thought I was going to have to say something, but Dr. Miller spoke up first.

"And how did you get access to open the case and take out the sword?"

Arthur looked up then, looking a little confused. Then his expression cleared.

"Oh. I didn't. I mean… you don't need access to take out the sword. Anyone can get into that case."

The head interrupted.

"Would you show us how, Arthur?"

Arthur hesitated, then rose and walked around the table. He stepped up onto the platform and crossed to the cabinet on the back wall. He grabbed it by either side and tugged.

It made a horrible screech as it slid forward about four inches, the bolts at its corners pulled partway from the plaster, then it stopped. He stuck his arm in between the cabinet and the sword, which was attached to the wall behind, and paused, looking back over his shoulder.

"Do you want me to take it out?"

"No, Arthur," said the head. "Just take your seat at the table."

That was the one thing I hadn't been able to figure out: how anyone but Pastor Dean could get the sword out of the case.

I addressed my request to the head.

"May I ask Arthur a question?"

Dr. Miller started to object, but the head paid him no attention.

"Please do. I want to hear it."

I waited for Arthur to sit.

"Can you tell me, Arthur, why you moved the body?"

He squirmed a little.

"For the... the same reason they said earlier. To create more suspects."

"Yes. That would have made a lot of sense, if Pastor Dean had killed him, because if the murder happened in the chapel it would point to Pastor Dean. But it wouldn't point to *you*, Arthur."

I waited for that to sink in before continuing.

"Tell me if I'm right about this. I think you did it for the opposite reason. I think you did it to create *fewer* suspects. I think you moved it to the boys' dormitory because that was the one place on campus that someone couldn't go."

I looked over my shoulder at Dolores. Our eyes met, and I watched her throw off her stupor with a visible effort.

She stood up, still returning my gaze.

"Adam's right," she said. "Arthur is trying to take the blame for me."

Dr. Brine spoke for the first time since he had called the session to order.

"I suppose, if we, ahhh, if we stay here much longer we'll have the entire school sitting at this table."

Chapter 10

"Then young Adam, though only a small child, stood before the judge and the assembly and spoke. One by one, he dismantled the arguments of the evil prosecutors, and piece by piece he assembled the facts until they formed an unassailable picture of the truth. All assembled were in awe of the wisdom shown by one so young, and none could find any fault in his speech. And the chief prosecutor was himself convicted of the crime, and the innocent man set free."

Anonymous,
Young Heroes of the Short Domination

I HAD BEEN VERY MUCH afraid that the head would see where my argument was headed and would try to stop it before it reached his daughter.

I was pretty sure I had used up his good will by now.

Dolores came forward to the table, sat down by Arthur, and began to talk before anyone asked a question. She started by addressing Arthur.

"It's very... *noble* of you to try to take the blame, Arthur, but it's not right."

She looked up at Dr. Brine.

"I was so scared, you see. The blood, and the sword sticking through him like that. I didn't *intend* for that to happen. And Arthur came in, and I begged him not to tell anyone—I think mostly I meant Daddy—and he just sort of took charge.

"He did all the things he said he did, with the rug and the rags and all, but he didn't kill him. He even pulled the sword out and wiped it off and put it back in the case."

I sneaked a glance at the head. He was in misery.

I couldn't let this go on.

"Dolores," I said, "did you stab Flash with the sword?"

She stopped and looked at me, then her eyes shifted toward her father.

"Oh." One hand rose involuntarily to cover her mouth. "Oh, *no* Daddy. I didn't *stab* him."

"So we're back to Pastor Dean," said Dr. Miller.

No one paid him any attention.

"But you said you killed him," said Arthur.

Her eyes shifted back to his.

"I only meant that it was my *fault*. That if I, if I..."

"Hadn't shown him how to open the case?" I prompted.

She nodded. "I showed him the night before. He had this thing, he called it a 'universal key,' and he tried to open it with that. And when it didn't work, I had to show off and tell him how to get in without it..."

Dolores, who'd had the run of the seminary her whole life, who knew about the dumb waiter and a thousand other quirks of these old buildings, would know there was a way to open the case without access.

She continued her story.

"I found him like that when I came in, lying there with the sword sticking right through him."

"Exactly," said Dr. Miller. "Just the way Pastor Dean left him."

No one seemed to be objecting to me talking anymore, so I pressed on.

"Dr. Brine," I said, "Do you remember when I told you I knew what Flash wanted to talk to Pastor Dean about?"

"Yes. As I... as I recall, you were quite unwilling to, ahhh, enlighten us on that matter."

"Well, I think I ought to tell you now."

"Better late than... Go ahead."

I took a deep breath.

"Dr. Miller preached a sermon a while ago, on the unforgivable sin. It was a very effective sermon, very powerful. And Flash took it to heart. He believed that he had committed the unforgivable sin. That he had cut himself off from God, and goodness, and everything worthwhile in life, and that he would spend eternity in Hell.

"He came to me, and I didn't know what to tell him. Eventually I suggested that he talk to Pastor Dean about it."

Dr. Miller cleared his throat.

"I don't see what this has to do with—"

"That wasn't all. Dr. Miller preached another sermon just two days ago, on the death of King Saul. The verse he preached from is still up there on the scripture board."

Dolores gave a little gasp at that. I forged on.

"Dr. Miller stressed in that sermon that Saul's beloved son died because of Saul's sin. And Flash was very worried about that. He thought *his* sin might cause someone he cared a great deal about to suffer if he didn't do something. So he did. He killed himself."

Dr. Miller interrupted me.

"I think this speculation has gone far enough. Do you have one bit of evidence that this was a suicide?"

This was the moment of truth, but I had plenty of reason to believe I was right.

"I don't, sir. But I believe someone else has."

I turned to Dolores.

"You weren't supposed to meet Flash in the chapel last night, were you?"

Her eyes got wide as she realized what I meant.

"No. We met here the night before, but he said he couldn't come last night."

"So why did you come here?"

"I was worried about Flash. Because I'd shown him how to get to the sword, and because of the message he sent me."

"What did it say?"

She opened her Bible, and after a moment she read it out loud.

"Dolores, I love you. Don't blame yourself. It's because of me, because of stuff that happened before we really knew each other. I have to do this. Logia 12:10, I Samuel 31:4."

I couldn't believe my luck—he'd actually used the texts.

"The texts from Dr. Miller's sermons," I said. "The first one is about the unforgivable sin. The second one is about King Saul's death."

And then I quoted the end of the verse.

"Therefore Saul took a sword and fell upon it."

Dr. Brine ruled that there was not enough evidence to hold Pastor Dean responsible for Flash's death, which I thought was a pretty mean-spirited way of saying he clearly didn't do it.

But Dr. Miller wasn't ready to give up.

"That," he said, "resolves the first question before us. But there remains the question of Pastor Dean's affair with a married woman."

I didn't have anything to say on that subject at all, and the truth is I felt pretty helpless. After all I had done, it still looked like they were going to find a way to hurt him—maybe even send him to that hermitage for the rest of his life.

But then help came from a completely unexpected direction.

"Oh, *that!*" Dolores exclaimed. "I explained all that to Flash."

She was suddenly the center of attention.

"Explained it?" her father said.

"It was so silly," she said. "He told me what he saw, and I told him it didn't mean a thing. I was so surprised he didn't *know.*"

"What did he see, Dolores?"

"He saw him hugging *Mom.* Out on the patio one night. They were talking, and when they were through he kissed her and gave her a hug."

The head and Pastor Dean looked at each other, suppressing smiles.

Dr. Brine was puzzled.

"I'm not, ahhh, quite sure *why*... why that exculpates—"

"Because, Dr. Brine," the head replied, "Sam—Pastor Dean —is my brother-in-law. My wife is his sister."

Dr. Brine declared the inquiry over, and people began filtering out of the pews and into the hallway. Dr. Miller and Dr. Brine were clearly not happy with the outcome, but good manners—or at least a pretense of good manners—forced them to drop by our end of the table and express their regrets for what they had put Pastor Dean through.

I was feeling pretty clever and pretty triumphant in the moment, so that's probably why I did what I did next. I certainly wouldn't have dared on another day.

Just as they were getting ready to leave I turned to Pastor Dean and spoke, loud enough for them to clearly hear me.

"Oh, Pastor Dean! With all the excitement, I forgot to tell you!"

"Tell me what?"

"Those initials I asked you about for my history assignment —O.C.S? The source you gave me—Wikipedia—had a whole list of possibilities: Officer Candidate School, Obsessive Compulsive Syndrome, Outer Continental Shelf, and more I haven't had time to sort through. So I should be able to find the one that fits."

As I said all that I saw understanding slowly creep into his eyes. He gave me a brief smile.

"I'm glad I could help."

Dr. Brine gave Dr. Miller a sharp look of disapproval, and stalked away. Dr. Miller hurried after him.

SEPARATION OF CASES

Chapter 11

"We all experience our dark hours, and when we are in them they can seem to deny even the possibility of light, but the thing to do in those moments is to persevere, to move on in search of the dawn."

Adam Kinde,
The Collected Sermons of Adam Kinde

THE SERVICE for Flash was held the next morning, instead of Sunday chapel. His friends came forward one by one and said what a great guy he was, what wonderful touchdowns he had made on the football field, how funny he had been teasing the angel, pranking the teachers, and so on.

I stayed in my seat. I knew a completely different Flash than they did. If I had talked about him, it would just have confused everyone. Besides, my connection with him was too personal somehow. Though I never thought of him as a friend, I suspected he talked to me about a lot of things he never mentioned to any of them.

But the main thing was what we had shared, even if I'd never mentioned it to Flash—the knowledge that we were doomed. I wouldn't expect any of them to understand that, or how it changed everything.

So I was a bit surprised when Pastor Dean brought it up.

He stepped into the pulpit after the last of Flash's friends had spoken and just stood there for a long time, his eyes roaming over everyone in the room. And then, when he began his voice was low and almost conversational.

"Every one of us, every one of you out there, is many different people in one body. And so was Flash. Those of us who knew him each knew a different Flash. I can't speak to them all in the few moments I have here, but I'd like to say a word about just three of the Flashes you may have known.

"The first Flash is the one you've just heard a lot about. The good friend, the athlete, the humorist, the leader. I don't have a lot to add to what they've said about that Flash, except to tell you that it is all true. You may not have ever known that Flash, but he was real, he did exist, and those you have just heard speak did know him.

"The second Flash I want to speak about is the bully. The Flash who terrified some of you, made you feel small, and whom some of you hated. That Flash was real, as well. Those of you who spoke earlier may not want to hear that, or to believe it, but it is true. I won't ask you, today in your grief over a lost friend, to examine yourselves to see if there may be a bully in you, but I will ask you to believe that some people here did know the bully in Flash.

"And I have something to say to those of you who were bullied, as well. You may not be able to mourn Flash with his friends. You may not find any great sadness within you over his death. When we mourn we're not sad for the person who is gone. We're sad for our own loss. You may not feel any loss. That is normal, and to be expected. It's enough that you are sensitive to those who *do* feel a loss.

"The third Flash I want to speak about is the Flash that most of you heard about in the inquiry yesterday. That's the Flash who believed that he had committed the unforgivable sin, that he had lost any connection to the holy and was doomed for all eternity.

"It's almost certain that there are some sitting here right now who believe the same thing of themselves. I did, for a time, when I was your age, and probably at least a third of all your teachers did as well. It's a very tempting thing to believe.

"But believing it doesn't make it true. I can't tell you whether Flash was right or not. I don't know the details. And even if I did, I *can* tell you that—in spite of what you may have heard from this pulpit on other occasions—there isn't any complete agreement about exactly what that sin may be, or what it takes to commit it. So it is entirely possible that Flash is in heaven at this moment. No mere human knows for sure.

"So let us stand, as a community, and bow our heads in silence for a moment over the grief of those who are grieving, after which I'll close in prayer."

AFTER THE PRAYER I stayed in my seat while the others filed out. Pastor Dean's words had only reminded me about my condition. He was right, of course, that I couldn't be one hundred percent certain, but the possibility was still all too real, and my own uncertainty was still there.

I just sat still, sort of numb, in the chapel where so much of it had happened. Where Dr. Miller had preached on the death of Judas while I thought about Dolores's request, where I had come in the middle of the night to find the bloody sword, where Dolores had shown Flash how to open the cabinet, where he had killed himself, and where the inquest and the service had been held.

After a while I became aware that Dolores was sitting beside me.

She was staring at the cabinet on the wall.

"It was all my fault," she said, and a tear ran down her cheek. "I don't know how to go on."

It took me a moment to pull myself out of the depths of my own problems and focus on her. When I was about to speak she continued.

"I just feel so... so *guilty*."

She turned to look a me, and her face crumpled with misery.

I searched my mind for something to say, something that might really help.

"Do you remember that conversation we had? The one when you asked me to find out if Flash liked you?"

She nodded.

"Well I already knew about the problem—the sin he believed he committed—before we talked that time. It was before you and he were even together."

"But you said, at the inquest when you were talking about his death, you said that he was afraid someone he cared about would suffer. Was that me?"

"Look. I said that because I had to get them to see that it wasn't Pastor Dean."

"But was it me? Was he worried about me?"

I relented.

"He *was* worried about you being involved, but honestly nothing he said about that implied that he would—"

"And I was the one who showed him how to get the sword. He might never have even thought of the sword if we hadn't met in the chapel to..."

She stopped, embarrassed.

"Listen Dolores, you're right that he cared about you and was worried about you. And I can't deny that you are the one who told him how to get the sword. But it's not a sin to have someone care about you, and you had no idea why he wanted to get into that case. You could have done the same thing a thousand times without anything bad coming of it. Right?"

She shook her head.

"He's still dead. And he wouldn't be if it weren't for me."

And then I had an idea.

"Dolores, have you ever heard of 'separation of cases'?"

"Separation of...?"

"Cases. It's something we're studying in logic class. There are only two possibilities, two cases, right? Either his death was your fault, or it wasn't."

"I guess so..."

"Okay. And you can't know for sure which is true, right?"

She thought about that one.

"Not for sure..."

"So," I said, "let's take them one at a time. What if it wasn't your fault? What should you do, then?"

"I don't know. I guess I'd be very sad that he's gone, and very sad for him—that he felt he had to do that."

"And how would you go on?"

"Well, I guess I just would. I'd have to."

"Okay. Now let's suppose that it *was* your fault. Was it on purpose?"

"Oh! No, of course not. I would never..."

"So what would you feel then? Sadness?"

"I guess, yes."

"And sad for him, that he felt he had to do that?"

"Yes."

"And how would you go on?"

It took her a moment, and then her voice was very quiet.

"I guess I'd just *have* to."

"Right. So you don't know, you can never know for sure, but in the end it leads to the same thing."

She sighed.

"You're right, I guess. But it's hard."

"Yes," I agreed. "It's hard."

***

AFTER DOLORES LEFT I sat there a while longer.

I thought about Flash, about Pastor Dean, and finally I thought about my own problem again.

It wasn't that different from Dolores's.

I'd either committed the unforgivable sin, or I hadn't.

I didn't *know*. I couldn't know for sure.

If I hadn't, it would be stupid to base the rest of my life on a false belief.

And if I had—if I were doomed to Hell after death—why should I make my own life Hell, here on Earth, by living any differently than I would have otherwise.

I could still choose to live just as if I hadn't committed it at all. I could have Heaven on Earth even if I'd lost it after death.

It came down to the same thing either way.

Separation of cases.

It was hard.

But I would go on.

***

Thank you for reading *The Human.*
Please visit krwatts.com to join my reader group.

I'll send you occasional updates about new releases, a free copy
of the book I'm currently giving to my readers, and other gifts.

All my best,
-krw

ALSO BY K. R. WATTS

The Guardian Dolphin

Parables from the Grave

ABOUT THE AUTHOR

K. R. Watts is the author of two series, *Philosophical Fantasies*, and the *Adam Kinde Alternate Future Mysteries*. He graduated from California State University at Northridge, and received an MA in theology and a Ph.D. in philosophy from Fuller Theological Seminary in Pasadena. He and his wife Virginia have two children and three grandchildren.